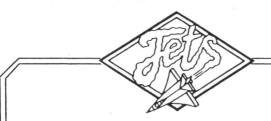

A Hiccup
on the High Seas

Karen Wallace

Collins

Best Friends · *Jessy and the Bridesmaid's Dress* · *Jessy Runs Away* · **Rachel Anderson**
Changing Charlie · *Clogpots in Space* · **Scoular Anderson**
Ernest the Heroic Lion-tamer · *Ivana the Inventor* · **Damon Burnard**
Weedy Me · **Sally Christie**
Almost Goodbye Guzzler · *Two Hoots* · **Helen Cresswell**
Magic Mash · *Nina's Machines* · **Peter Firmin**
Clever Trevor · *The Mystery of Lydia Dustbin's Diamonds* · *Nora Bone* ·
Nora Bone and the Tooth Fairy · **Brough Girling**
Sharon and Darren · **Nigel Gray**
Thing-in-a-Box · *Thing-on-two-Legs* · **Diana Hendry**
Desperate for a Dog · *More Dog Trouble* · **Rose Impey**
Georgie and the Computer Bugs · *Georgie and the Dragon* ·
Georgie and the Planet Raider · **Julia Jarman**
Cowardy Cowardy Cutlass · *Free With Every Pack* · *Mo and the Mummy Case* ·
The Fizziness Business · **Robin Kingsland**
And Pigs Might Fly! · *Albertine, Goose Queen* · *Jigger's Day Off* ·
Martians at Mudpuddle Farm · *Mossop's Last Chance* ·
Mum's the Word · **Michael Morpurgo**
Granny Grimm's Gruesome Glasses · **Jenny Nimmo**
Grubble Trouble · **Hilda Offen**
Hiccup Harry · *Harry on Holiday* · *Harry's Party* · *Harry the Superhero* ·
Harry with Spots On · **Chris Powling**
Grandad's Concrete Garden · **Shoo Rayner**
Rattle and Hum – Robot Detectives · *Rattle and Hum in Double Trouble* · **Frank Rodgers**
The Father Christmas Trap · **Margaret Stonborough**
Our Toilet's Haunted · **John Talbot**
Pesters of the West · **Lisa Taylor**
Jacko · *Lost Property* · *Messages* · **Pat Thomson**
A Hiccup on the High Seas · **Karen Wallace**
Monty, the Dog who Wears Glasses · *Monty Bites Back* · *Monty Ahoy!* ·
Monty Must be Magic! · *Monty up to his Neck in Trouble* ·
Monty's Ups and Downs · **Colin West**
Bing Bang Boogie, it's a Boy Scout · *Ging Gang Goolie, it's an Alien* · *Stone the Crows, it's a
Vacuum-cleaner* · **Bob Wilson**

First published by A & C Black (Publishers) Ltd 1997
Published by Collins in 1998

10 9 8 7 6 5 4 3 2

Collins is an imprint of HarperCollins Publishers Ltd,
77/85 Fulham Palace Road, London W6 8JB

Text copyright © 1997 Karen Wallace
Illustrations copyright © 1997 Russell Ayto
All rights reserved.

ISBN 0–00–675–323–X

Printed and bound in Great Britain by Clays Ltd, St Ives plc

Chapter One

Spike Lard
was a rude,
bad-tempered
Viking and
captain of the
Ruthless Rat.

Spike Lard was the kind
of Viking who gives
Vikings a bad name.

Gimme yer
gold or I'll
kick your ankles!

Crusty Choppers was a tough, kind-hearted Viking and captain of the *Dopey Duck*.

Crusty Choppers was the kind of Viking who gives Vikings a good name.

Spike Lard and Crusty Choppers
didn't like each other one bit.

The *Ruthless Rat* and the *Dopey
Duck* didn't like each other either.

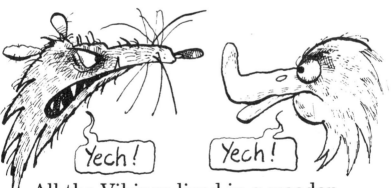

All the Vikings lived in a wooden
hall by the sea. In the winter it was
very cold. The only thing that kept
them warm was a fire-eating dragon.

One evening it was particularly icy.
As everyone sat down to a supper
of caribou and carrot soup, Spike
Lard suddenly grabbed a spear
and threw it at Crusty Choppers.

It hit the wall two inches from Crusty
Choppers' teeth.

Oi! Why should you have the

Crusty Choppers' face went black with anger. If there was one thing that made him really cross, it was bad manners.

The little fire-eating dragon opened a sleepy eye and sighed.

A lovely blast of warm air rolled all the way down the hall. Well, almost all the way. It stopped just short of Spike Lard.

'That wasn't very clever,' said Crusty's brother, Leafmould.

'You're a bunch of sissies,' yelled Harpoona, who was Spike's sister.

Things were getting out of hand. So Chief Thunder Ironfist bellowed: 'There will be no more squabbling!'

Chapter Two

At dawn the next day, Crusty and
Leafmould loaded up the *Dopey Duck*.

Leafmould wasn't a
very good sailor but
he was a keen
cook and loved
collecting recipes.
He always took a
recipe book and
a tasting spoon
on his voyages.

Perhaps I'll leave
my apron behind.

Beside them Spike and Harpoona were pulling up the anchor of the *Ruthless Rat*.

'Don't forget your tasting spoon!' sneered Harpoona. She waved a nasty-looking knife.

Crusty Choppers pulled up the sail.

We can look after ourselves, thank you.

As the sun rose, the two boats sailed away. For eight days and eight nights they ploughed through stormy seas. At first they headed south, then the *Dopey Duck* changed its mind and headed north.

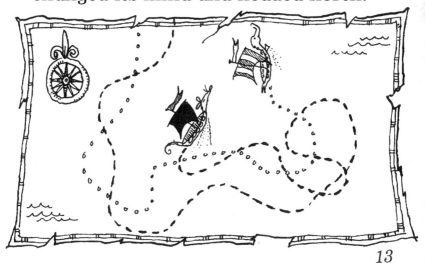

The *Ruthless Rat* followed behind because neither Spike nor Harpoona had remembered to pack a compass.

On the ninth day, as the evening stars came out, the two boats sailed into a bay.

On a rocky cliff above them, two huge bonfires were burning. A little further away there was a group of cottages.

15

The duck paused. Crusty waited.

So Crusty Choppers took down the
sails and lowered the anchor. Then
he wrapped himself in a blanket
and sank into a damp salty sleep.

That night he had the strangest
dream. He dreamed that the two
bonfires were not bonfires at all.

He dreamed that
they were two big
red eyes.

Chapter Three

The next day the sun came out, the sky was blue and the wind dropped.

After drinking a pot of fish head tea, Crusty tied his trusty little axe to his belt. Leafmould stuffed his recipe book into his tunic.

As they waded ashore, something that sounded like a seagull squeaked above them.

It squeaked again.

Help! Help!

Crusty and Leafmould looked up.
'Wobbling walruses!' cried Crusty
Choppers.

A tiny man was being dragged along
the edge of the cliff by a rope. The
rope was tied to a huge golden cow.

Crusty and Leafmould
watched as the cow
tossed her horns and
flipped the little man
over the edge.

'Help! Help!' screamed the man clinging on to the rope.

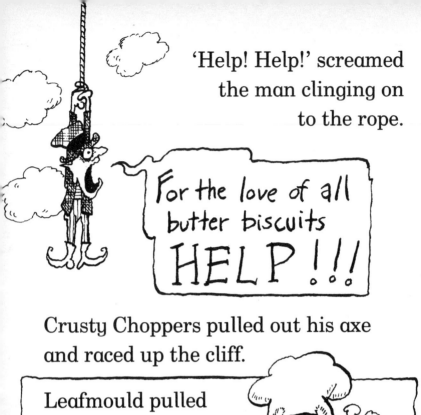

For the love of all butter biscuits HELP !!!

Crusty Choppers pulled out his axe and raced up the cliff.

Leafmould pulled out his book and looked under B. There was only a disgusting recipe for *Bog Stew*.

What on earth are biscuits?

Recipe Book

A new recipe!

Leafmould's pale face began to go pink with excitement.

By the time Leafmould reached the
top of the cliff, Crusty was running
along the path.
Ahead of him the
golden cow was
bellowing . . .

. . . and stamping
her feet.

Then she turned and saw Crusty.
It must have been the horns on
Crusty's helmet! The golden cow
went all quiet and soppy and batted
her eyelashes at him.

Crusty pulled up the rope and the little man scrambled on to the cliff.

A thousand thanks.

He was dressed in green from head to toe.

Dermot Puck-Patrick is the name. And I owe you the greatest of favours.

Crusty Choppers blushed. He wasn't used to people being so polite.

'You are in Ireland,' replied Dermot Puck-Patrick. He laughed and clapped his hands.

At that moment,
Leafmould appeared.

He turned and kissed
the golden cow.

A great rumbling of Viking stomachs shook the air. Dermot Puck-Patrick hooted with laughter.

Chapter Four

All that day, Dermot told stories about leprechauns and fairies and wizards. Crusty and Leafmould told stories about icebergs like crystal castles and whales like mountains.

Dermot gave Leafmould lots of recipes. In return Crusty Choppers chopped lots of wood with his trusty axe.

While Crusty and Leafmould were
having tea, Spike and Harpoona
were loading up the *Ruthless Rat*
with treasures.

Harpoona let out a yowl of laughter.
'And one more after that!'

The yowl bounced over the water,
up the cliff, and in through the
kitchen window to where Dermot
Puck-Patrick, Crusty and
Leafmould were sitting.

At the sound of Harpoona's voice,
Crusty blushed with shame.

Crusty Choppers
nearly choked on
his biscuit.

'The monster that lives under the cliff,' replied Dermot Puck-Patrick. He winked at Crusty.

A few moments later Crusty and Leafmould stood with their knees knocking at the edge of the cliff.

Crusty and Leafmould nodded – they were so frightened they couldn't speak.

They're not bonfires. They're the monster's eyes!

Dermot smiled and his eyes glowed with a strange green light.

Below them Crusty and Leafmould saw the *Ruthless Rat*. They heard nasty voices rising from the water.

'This monster,' said
Crusty Choppers
in a shaking voice.

Dermot Puck-Patrick spoke in a
high sing-song voice, as if he was
casting a spell.

Crusty Choppers didn't
know what to do.
Even though Spike
and Harpoona were
the rudest of raiders,

they were still
Vikings. And Vikings
should stick together.

I must
warn them.

And before anyone could stop him,
he pulled off his helmet and dived
into the sea.

Chapter Five

The first stars were just coming out
as Crusty Choppers reached the
side of the *Ruthless Rat*.

'Fat chance!' sneered Spike waving his hand at the sacks stacked inside the boat.

Out of the corner of his eye, Crusty saw a huge dark shadow moving steadily across the water.

Harpoona pushed him away with her paddle.

Suddenly a huge
scaly claw rose
out of the water.
At the same
moment, Crusty
Choppers felt
himself being
lifted high into
the air. He heard
Dermot Puck-
Patrick's voice
in his ears.
*'I owe you
the greatest
of favours,'*
it whispered.

Far below, the scaly claw twirled the
Ruthless Rat like a sausage on a spit.

All their sacks
of gold fell into
the sea.

Then it dragged the
Ruthless Rat down
into the swirling
black water.

When Crusty Choppers opened his eyes he was sitting on the beach. The *Ruthless Rat* was gone.

Crusty groaned. He saw Dermot's strange green eyes. He heard his strange sing-song voice. He stared at the empty water.

Crusty tried to remember if Spike and Harpoona had ever done anything nice. He couldn't think of anything.

There was a shout from above him. Leafmould was leading the golden cow down the cliff to the shore. A big sack was tied to its back. Leafmould's face was white as a candle.

'Dermot disappeared in a puff of smoke!' he cried.

And suddenly, there I was – holding the cow's rope and a sack of biscuits!

Crusty and Leafmould
stared at each other.

Leafmould nodded and the cow
mooed. As the three of them swam
back to the *Dopey Duck*, they heard
the most extraordinary sounds
coming from under the water.

It sounded like a monster with a
nasty taste in its mouth.

Chapter Six

'Could have been better, could have been worse,' quacked the duck when he heard the story.

But a cow and a recipe are not to be sneezed at.

As they prepared to set sail, the sea suddenly began to boil. There was a deep rumbling sound . . .

UGHUBBLE! AAARGUBBLE!

YECHUBBLE!

. . . then the air exploded with one gigantic watery

The *Ruthless Rat* shot out of the swirling sea and landed with a huge splash beside them. Harpoona threw back her matted black hair and hooted with laughter.

Bet you're Pleased to see us! We tasted so horrible the Monster spat us Out!

'And this is for Thunder Ironfist,' shouted Spike, waving a huge pointed tooth.

The next moment, *two* black sails billowed out from the front of the *Ruthless Rat!*

Harpoona waved something shiny
in her hands. It was the compass
that belonged to the *Dopey Duck*.

Crusty Choppers put his head in his hands.

Now what are we going to do?

We can't find our way home without a compass.

The *Dopey Duck* was not known for making fast decisions. But this time, something extraordinary happened.

44

'What on earth are you talking about?' shouted Crusty Choppers, whose patience had suddenly run out.

A great grin spread across Leafmould's face. After cooking, sewing was his favourite thing.

In no time at all . . .

. . . the *Dopey Duck* had a second sail of its own.

Crusty Choppers rolled his eyes and tried not to laugh.

Suddenly the wind filled the biscuit sack sail and the *Dopey Duck* shot off after the *Ruthless Rat*.

Chapter Seven

For seven days and seven nights, the *Dopey Duck* rode the sea with their biscuit sack sail but not once did they catch a glimpse of the *Ruthless Rat*.

On the eighth day, Leafmould climbed up the mast.

At that
moment
a huge wave
lifted the *Dopey
Duck* into
the air.

The *Ruthless Rat* was just in front
of them! And the land of Vikings
was just beyond! The two boats
raced over the water.

But no matter how he tried . . .

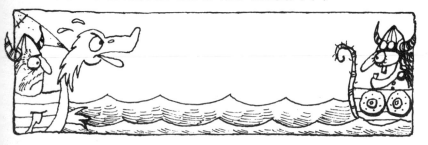

. . . the *Dopey Duck* could not catch up with the *Ruthless Rat*.

The two boats drew nearer and nearer to the shore. A crowd of Vikings were waiting. They cheered and waved their spears. And in the middle stood the Chief of all the Vikings – Thunder Ironfist.

Harpoona cupped her hands
around her mouth.

Too bad,
Sissies.
Only real raiders
win races.

She picked up Spike's long spear
and twirled it in the air.

RRRRRRIP!

Oops!

The spear
went straight
through the
Ruthless Rat's
secret sail and
tore it in half.

The *Ruthless Rat* slowed down.

The *Dopey Duck* caught up.

The two boats landed on the shore at exactly the same time!

'Spike Lard!' bellowed Thunder Ironfist.

What is the greatest prize aboard the *Ruthless Rat*?

The crowd of Vikings roared and
rattled their spears. This was
indeed a tremendous prize!

'Crusty Choppers!' cried
Thunder Ironfist.

What is the greatest prize aboard the Dopey Duck?

Crusty Choppers looked at the
sea-sick cow lying upside
down at the bottom
of his boat.
His heart sank.

The crowd of Vikings threw down
their spears and fell about laughing.
The *Dopey Duck* had truly lived up
to its name this time.

Thunder Ironfist raised his spear.
Such an important decision could
not be taken lightly.

Chapter Eight

That evening Spike Lard strutted about the great hall showing off his monster's tooth.

'When the *Ruthless Rat* wins,' he cried, prodding the fire-eating dragon with his foot, 'I shall keep this sooty serpent at my end of the room.'

The little dragon sneezed and burnt a hole in Spike Lard's shoe.

At that moment, Leafmould and Crusty Choppers came into the hall. They carried two jugs of the finest milk and a huge tray stacked with golden butter biscuits.

They placed the food in front of Thunder Ironfist.

At the first bite, a murmur of astonishment rippled down the table.

mmm mm m m mm!

Everyone declared they were the sweetest, most crumbly things they had ever tasted.

Everyone except for Spike and Harpoona. They were busy squabbling over the monster's tooth.

Give it back!!

No!!!

At last the time came for Thunder
Ironfist to make his announcement.

A monster's
tooth is indeed
a great prize.

And I'm
told it makes
very good
soup.
But...

He stuffed the last
biscuit into his mouth.

...these
things are, um,
well, these crisp,
crumbly, crunchy,
buttery...

For the first time, Thunder Ironfist, Chief of all the Vikings, was lost for words. Had he forgotten what Leafmould called these delicious things?

Everyone fell silent.

Even the fire-eating dragon held its breath.

Thunder Ironfist wiped his mouth
with his sleeve.

Everyone stomped their feet and
cheered. Crusty Choppers and
Leafmould went pink with delight.

The little fire-eating dragon heaved a huge sigh of relief and a wonderful blast of hot air rolled all the way down the room. *Ahhh!*

Well, almost all the way. It stopped just short of Spike and Harpoona.

But they didn't even notice.

They were too busy fighting.

Spike Lard had **stolen** the monster's tooth!